I0522578

DEVIANT-HUNTER'S SABBATH

AN EVE OF LIGHT STORY

HARAMBEE K. GREY-SUN

This book is a work of fiction. Names, characters, places, and incidents are the products of the author's imagination or are used fictitiously. Any resemblance to actual events, locales, or persons, living or dead, is entirely coincidental.

Copyright © 2015, 2018 by Harambee K. Grey-Sun

All rights reserved. No part of this book may be reproduced in any form or by any means, including scanning, photocopying, or otherwise without the expressed written consent or permission from the publisher or author, except in the case of a reviewer, who may quote brief passages embodied in critical articles or in a review.

Cover design by The Cover Collection.

Print ISBN-13: 978-1-64044-009-8

Ebook ISBN-13: 978-1-64044-008-1

Second Edition: June 2018

Published by HyperVerse Books, LLC

www.hyperversebooks.com

Crossing genres without apologies.

1

—————

The dark-amber liquid was silk on my tongue. I knew many connoisseurs preferred *velvet* as their catchword, but as I sipped, I briefly had the impression of ravishing Carolyn, stripping her of her negligee, using only my mouth.

I rubbed the tip of my tongue across my upper and lower lip, pursed them, then *smacked*. No one else in the bar noticed, but I wouldn't have given a damn if they had. It couldn't be helped. Twenty-year-old tawny this good deserved a kiss—as did the memory of my wife, ten years gone.

The Sweet & Smoky had a decent mix of regulars and irregulars this afternoon. No more than two dozen or so, total. Average capacity for an early Friday afternoon. All of them were here to chat and relax over port or cigars or both. They had no other options in this little nook of heaven.

I was relaxing but had no interest in chatting with anyone. This week had played hell with my stamina and my sensibilities. My body was almost back to where it needed to be, but I needed a bit more time to get my mind right before the next hunt.

Time, however, had never been my pal.

I almost met the eyes of the deviant as he walked in. Lucky me: my specs weren't on the right setting. I saw the aura about his head, but my eyes weren't protected from any electromagnetic glare he might give me. I glanced away in time as he scanned the seating area; he was searching for more of his kind, I was sure. Finding none, he made his way to the bar.

I'd been careful when choosing my seat, as usual—dark corner, back against the wall. I'd no chance of staying completely hidden from those who could see through the dark and stuff much more solid. I just didn't want any of the bastards sneaking up on me.

This one wasn't stealthy at all, but he did take risks. His kind took a risk with each swallow of alcohol. I presumed he was among those on one of the stronger medications. The first clue was the way he carried himself.

He hadn't run in like a lunatic, frothing at the mouth while raving rhymes and puns. He wasn't a singer or dancer, trying to boil brains with a voice or slice throats with wicked moves. Not a would-be artist. He was seemingly just another smug hipster.

I knew the truth. I wouldn't take my eyes off him. I'd try my damnedest to not even blink. None of the deviants were to be trusted.

This one slid up to the bar like a room-temp ice cube. I adjusted my specs and gave him a good look, just to be sure. My special status with the Heartland Security Agency notwithstanding, I couldn't afford to make a mistake.

Yeah . . . I picked up the telltale signs—the dirty little mites, like several hundred miniscule bits of foil reflecting a variety of unnamable colors, off and on, like sparkles as they traveled complicated highways just under the upper layers of his skin. I downed my glass and stood up.

Most of my gear was in The Machine—under the seats, in the glove compartment, and in the back. Aside from my specs, which appeared to onlookers as the latest in sports-goggle fashion, I had two or three Skrapnel capsules on me, two eggs of Pixie Dust, one syringe, and a pair of sturdy gloves. I was wearing my custom leather shoulder holster, but it was empty. I carried no firearms, as guns and alcohol didn't mix well with me. Either way, I couldn't do anything in the Sweet & Smoky even if I wanted to. Not that I wanted to. I liked this bar. Quality port and the best cigars to be found in North Carolina—what was not to like?

The occasional clientele, I supposed. The target had struck up a conversation with Ed, the bartender. Ed shifted his eyes for just a second or less, catching my approach. Neither his voice nor his demeanor betrayed him, and his body language remained silent. It didn't matter. His eyes told the whole story in a flicker. The deviant, like most others of his kind, probably knew something was up before he saw me take my place at the bar, two stools down from him. Wasn't Ed's fault. The gloves would've given me away anyway. Few people had a reason to wear fire-resistant gloves with integrated knuckles in here; I rarely had a reason to take them off.

"Another twenty-year tawny," I said, interrupting whatever tale the deviant had been telling Ed.

Ed edged away a step at a time, keeping his eyes on the deviant, pretending to still be engrossed in the story, until the target finally stopped talking.

"Better get the man his drink," the deviant said. He'd

gotten the hint. "I can finish the story later, if you're still interested."

"I'm interested," I said as Ed turned to retrieve the bottle.

The deviant glared with his eyes but smiled with his lips.

I adjusted my specs, setting the filter, before meeting his stare. I didn't want his mind entering mine. But I briefly wondered what he thought, getting a look at this unshaven man with receding hair at least twenty years his senior. I probably still smelled a little of the grass I'd cut this morning—I didn't know—but he seemed amused.

"Any idea what I was going on about?" he asked.

"I can guess," I said as Ed returned with my port. "Your life story. A dirty *joke*. Whichever—the funny's usually the same." I held the glass up to my nose.

"Oh yeah?" He shifted, turning his body toward me. I knew his story in just a few glances. He was wearing yellow work boots in which he'd never performed a minute's worth of work, torn and faded jeans recently purchased from a local thrift store, an open plaid shirt with the sleeves rolls up to his elbows, and a black T-shirt with some cartoon etched in white that I was just hip enough to recognize as ironic. Normally I wouldn't even need my special tools; a round from my P320 could end him in a second. But respecting Ed's wishes to run a respectable establishment, I never brought it or any other piece inside the S & S.

While I studied him, the deviant studied me further: in the jeans I'd roughed up and patched up all by myself over the last several years, in the boots that had been through actual combat, and the softshell jacket, which was water repellant, wind resistant, and specially modified to hold and hide a few accessories.

His smile faded as our faces traded expressions.

"Maybe you'd like to pick up where I left off," he said flatly.

"Sure," I said. "Your story is the one of a naughty boy, one who should've left it alone instead of picking it up and playing with it." His brow furrowed as I said, "Now, I know you're no moralist, so your life story doesn't have a good moral or even a good laugh. But I can finish it in such a way that it has *both*."

He sniffed. "You're neither clever nor funny, hick."

I nodded toward the entrance. "Let's step outside. I promise I'll leave you in stitches."

"Go fuck yourself." The deviant threw some money on the bar, gathered his cigars, and retreated to the lounge area, where the majority of the smokers were.

I held my glass and stood as I watched him settle into a comfortable leather chair.

With narrowing eyes, he watched me approach. He bit off the end of one cigar as I took the armchair adjacent to his. I expected him to spit it at me, but it hit the floor right before he said, "What do you want, prick? A date?"

I nodded. "How 'bout this evening?"

"Just leave me the fuck alone." He lit up the cigar—with a match, not his vision.

"You see, that's the thing. I can't. You and your kind are fucking up my kind, spreading your disease, corrupting bodies and minds, polluting every environment God and Mother Nature blessed humankind with—an environment in which we were supposed to thrive, excel, eventually transcend our own skin . . ."

"Oh." He puffed, then sneered. "You're one of those. Of course."

I smiled and moved my right hand closer to my heart. "I've pledged my allegiance."

"A nut," the deviant said. "A fundamentalist, in a bar. I shouldn't be surprised."

Oddly, his pupils didn't shift; his irises didn't change color; he didn't even *try* to X-ray my jacket pockets.

"At least," he continued, "my surprise shouldn't equal my disgust at seeing a religious type with a drink in his hand, preaching to and against someone he knows nothing about. Blow away, reverend redneck. Let me smoke and think in peace."

"Here's something you should think about, deviant." I leaned forward. "I do believe in family. I do believe in God. I believe in angels, the *true* angels: twenty-first-century humans at their true potential. I believe a fraction of these would-be angels have fallen from grace—*hard*—and I believe you're among that tainted elite."

He remained sitting, comfortably leaning backward, but I was perceptive enough to tell all the swagger had left his body. Cocksure no more, he was at a loss as to what to say. Maybe it was my words or merely my grin. Or maybe, reading the body language, he was smart enough to tell mine was winning the argument. Whichever, he felt he had only one tactic left.

The deviant leaned forward and puffed, blowing cigar smoke in my face.

No, he was in no way *smart*.

Coming from a man, this would have been a minor annoyance, like a death-wishing clown throwing confetti into my face. But as with any deviant, my senses were on high alert. The odor was like brimstone; the smoke was denser than London fog. Even though my specs were set to automatically adjust and cut through it, when they did, he was gone.

Well, not really. Just invisible.

I stood as I manually adjusted the specs and looked around. *Got 'im.* He was walking quickly toward the exit. I moved at twice the pace.

"Frank..." Ed called.

I waved him off. I wasn't stopping. Did he really think I would let one that fell into my lap get away—*run* away—to unleash yet a little more Hell on Earth?

The deviant was heading toward a vehicle: a late-model hybrid. *Funny.*

I reached in my jacket and retrieved a Skrapnel capsule from the pocket near my left shoulder. I then stopped, reared back, and shouted, "Hey—you forgot this!"

He slowed and turned, perhaps involuntarily, just a bit but just enough. The capsule had already left my hand. He may've realized what it was a fraction of a second before it pegged him, bursting open on his left cheek.

He transitioned to visibility as he screamed at a pitch that would've curdled the blood of those with hides much thinner than mine.

The parking lot was empty. The only folks who heard were those across the street. Like all smart citizens in this day and age, they scurried away from any sign of trouble, paying it only a glance.

I kept running, adjusting my specs and reaching in the other side of my jacket for the "pen" holsters.

The minuscule metal jacks that had managed to attach themselves to the deviant's cheek were melting and being absorbed as if the skin were cloth seeping up water. The Skrapnel would hopefully do its job, preventing the thing from using its light-manipulating abilities, or at least making it damn painful to do so.

I'd been lucky enough to hit the face. That was prime property on any deviant's body. But this one wasn't as stupid as I was ready to presume. His face remained, anguished expression and all, as the patterns on his clothes shifted, first to a three-dimensional plaid and then to something unexplainable, appearing in shape like a hovering stingray, one with the same color as television snow with a few blotches of red thrown in.

I'd faced stuff more bizarre. I took the syringe out of the "pen" holster and continued forward.

He ran, too—*toward* me, yelling a war cry of sorts. The cries of these deviants were sometimes simply meant to intimidate. Oftentimes, the sounds were used as weapons.

My initial impression of static wasn't far off as I heard a crunchy roar, popping on every part of my outer, middle, and inner ears as it went deeper to whip snap my nerves. I wasn't quite ready for it.

On a better day, I would've done better than stumble and trip, almost jabbing the syringe filled with liquid metal into my own chest. I tossed it aside, under a car, before falling and scuffing up my jeans as I pushed myself up and kept moving. I'd been trained to never remain still when facing off against their kind, no matter how much it hurt.

If only I'd parked closer to the building, I would've bolted for my Hummer. But the former agent in me was always prodding to park far away, at a good enough distance to do surveillance on the way to the end point. Lot of good it did me at this point.

Separated from The Machine, the best I could hope to do was run headlong into the deviant, tackle him, and strangle him till he lost consciousness. The target was already bleeding on his cheek, but maybe I could finesse him down so that the blood wouldn't touch me or anyone else, and I wouldn't shed more.

Easier thought than accomplished.

The staticky stingray with the pissed-off man's head was as elusive as he appeared, and he had something sharp I couldn't see. When we were close to colliding, I dove and missed, but he rapidly sliced up the forearms of my jacket. As I pushed up from the asphalt, I noticed he'd gotten deep enough to draw blood.

Damn. The mission earlier in the week must've taken a bigger toll than I'd thought. I was much better than all this. Forget the deviant's blood touching my skin; if it touched my *blood* . . .

I stood and whirled around. He was there, ready to grab my arms, ready to dance the last one.

I clasped my hands behind my back and kicked—a child's move, but I wasn't interested in proving my maturity. The tip of my composite-toe boot didn't connect with his groin or any other chunk of flesh, just visual snow. I expected it—I'd made the move only to make him pause while I shifted my weight back and to the side, hitting the ground and rolling for a few feet, putting distance between us as I reached inside my jacket for the egg close to my heart.

He saw. This time it was fear rather than confusion that kept him in one place. He wasn't a skilled combatant; otherwise, he would've moved when I fastballed the egg straight toward his face.

There was no war cry this time. It was more of a *death scream* as the sun's rays connected with the granules that stuck to the deviant's skin like damp sugar crystals. They were nothing any human would ever want to ingest, but the sun's rays shaved themselves down to the thinnest, tiniest, sharpest snakelike devourers, eating, ingesting, and immediately processing the crystals as, in turn, the parasites in the deviant's skin and blood fed on the electromagnetic rays, attempting to digest and process but only regurgitating them. I wasn't seeing it down to the exact details; this is how it had been described to me back when I was with the Agency. But I didn't even really need my special-agent specs to see the deviant's head being picked apart by the hair of a sun-Medusa, picked to the bone, leaving a blood-streaked, crystallized skull in its place.

Curious and brave patrons poured out of the S & S in time to see the deviant's lifeless body slump and a piece of its prism-patched skull chip off when it hit the pavement.

I heard the expected groans and screams as I hustled to The Machine, uncloaked it, and opened the back. I had only two of the specially lined body bags left. I'd need to restock first thing in the morning.

I put on a different jacket and a surgeon's face mask. I wished I could've donned my battle-dress uniform, but I didn't have the time—and if I wanted to maintain my "special" status, that was a no-no in this environment. This wasn't the woods or countryside. I couldn't even put on my helmet.

Once my skin was covered as much as possible, I pulled out my cell and called one among my most-trusted at the Agency as I doubled back to the remains. Thankfully, no one had been brave or stupid enough to approach it, so there was no need to shoo or shout anyone away.

I finished my call and visually examined the body, adjusting my specs several times. The thing was dead, but I wanted to be sure there'd be no convulsions or other surprises when I touched the body. I was mostly covered, but I didn't want to leave anything to chance.

There were still living parasites in the corpse, but they'd been shocked to exhaustion. I went to work.

I'd no trouble zipping him up.

My Agency contact promised to send a retrieval squad to take the body and handle damage control for the witnesses. They'd probably use the same old story about the guy trying to rob the place. Ed would go along. He'd been a great friend throughout the years. I just hoped the damn squad got here soon.

I checked my watch. School was almost out.

2

―――――

Frankie was her usual talkative self on the way home. I almost offered to stop by a Dairy Queen, but a cold tongue would only slow her down, not keep her quiet. I wondered about the other parents I'd occasionally met in the Sweet & Smoky, those who complained about the communication skills, or lack thereof, of their teenage sons. I was the only single dad I knew who was bringing up a girl still in her early tweens. When she hit high school in three years, would she be a motormouth, running even faster than now, or would she be as tightlipped as I was at that age?

"And then she said I was fat, and a slut, and I'd never get—"

"Wait, *what*?" I almost slammed on the brakes.

"Jenny said I was—"

"*Frankie*, that language is not appropriate for you. I don't ever want to hear you say that again, you understand?"

"What word?"

"The *S*-one."

"Why?"

I sighed. "It refers to inappropriate behavior."

"Like what?"

"Like . . . if you do too much of one thing, something you shouldn't be doing, you get called that word."

"What one thing? Sex?"

"*Frankie—*"

"Like, how if someone eats too much, they're fat? Maybe I do eat too much. Maybe Jenny's right. She *is* my best friend. And fat kinda rhymes with slut, but—"

Carolyn . . . I needed her now more than ever.

The dear woman had died shortly before our daughter reached the terrible twos—a hit-and-run. She'd been crossing the street with Frankie, who'd miraculously survived, though her face had gotten scratched up a bit. It was nothing some minor surgery couldn't fix. And with the help of some Agency resources, I found and fixed the guy who was responsible for it all, but it didn't bring me peace. And Frankie had seemed stuck in an odd phase ever since. Smart as a whip when it came to making the grades, she did her chores when asked, and she never acted out. But she babbled like a brook. It wasn't ADD. I was sure it was some kind of posttraumatic response to witnessing her mother being murdered and just barely surviving death herself.

Psychiatric help might be in order at some point, though I knew within moments of me taking her to see any headshrink, the doc would probably be more interested in me than her. Waste of time and money, even if I could get the Agency to pay for it.

I steered The Machine onto the long, curving driveway that had home as its end point, hidden now by the copious amounts of loblollies that surrounded the property. About a third of the way in, I reached up to the console nestled between the visors and punched in a code. This ensured at the halfway point, when the gate automatically opened (as it did for any vehicle), only my particular vehicle would be allowed easy passage. Anything else—on wheels or two feet, seen or unseen—would set off an alarm both in my house and in The Machine. But I heard nothing other than Frankie's motormouth as the beautiful, expansive Tudor came into view. Carolyn had always loved this house. And it was only thanks to her family that we had been able to afford it. It was thanks to my connections that it remained secure, if not as prettied up and well maintained as it had been when Carolyn was alive to crack the whip and ensure the outside remained as well kempt and pretty as it was inside.

Stopping the vehicle outside the garage, I again reached up to the console and punched in some necessary codes. The security system recognized two and only two persons exiting the vehicle. Anything more would trip another alarm. From time to time I'd gotten a few falsies, but they were rare. The house was about three-quarters of a mile away from any others. And I wasn't exactly the type to invite folks over for dinner or game night. I enjoyed my privacy and my safety. I had several devices—some in the vehicle, some in the house, and a few on my person at any given time—that linked up to the scanners in and around the property. They not only apprised me of danger while I was on the premises; I'd also know if there'd been unusual happenings or unwelcome visitors since I'd been gone.

Getting a clean report, I entered in another combination, this one to open the garage door. I pulled the vehicle in and shut off the engine, but Frankie hopped out before I could even shut the garage door. Though it was nowhere close to touching her, she dove, tucked, and rolled under the slow-closing door before hopping to her feet to dash out in to the yard, intending to chase squirrels or whatever. The girl needed a dog. Maybe I did too.

I'd heard many of the other "Designated Hitters" in Texas, California, Florida, and elsewhere highly preferred dogs over any other companions, including spouses. I corresponded with a few of these good men and women. Many were former domestic black ops like me. And like me, many had been fighting for ten years or more, either in direct service of the government or as private contractors assisting the authorities in a world that had changed more in ten years than it had in centuries—that is, if one knew how to see the unseen.

Race, class, nationality—none of that shit really mattered anymore. It was shortsighted to focus on such spurious divisions. We humans were all potential angels, all on the verge stepping up to the next level once we realized how blessed we were with our modern knowledge and technology. But our world was under attack—not by aliens from a distant star but by sinful people who'd grown up among us, licentious scumbags who'd acquired bizarre and incurable infections that somehow gave their bodies the ability to manipulate the properties of light and their minds a fixation on destroying our world.

Some evenings, I almost pined for the days of my late twenties. That time hadn't been stellar—we'd had a shithead as president, a wet-rag Congress, a willfully blind Supreme Court, and nations of bomb-wielding Neanderthals that wanted to wipe America off the face of the earth. And unlike too many others back then, I never much cared for judging folks solely by their accents or the color of their skin. But the world had been a bit more sensible. One could understand their place and devise strategies toward a better, brighter future. Then something tweaked wrong in the bodies and minds of a few careless people who chose to forfeit their humanity—body, mind, and *soul*. The world, for the most part, went on as before, except for those of us who'd had the misfortune of being on the front lines the day many took a fool's leap off the cliff, down into the abyss.

The God-is-dead Nietzschian assholes finally went too far, pushing the limits, and when they pulled out, the rest of us—the sober and staid, God-fearing humans—were left to deal with the glistening, slime-coated vermin. The rest of us weren't staring back at ourselves; we were staring at a multitude of Antichrists, some of whom may or may not have had help from some folks deep in the swamp of Washington.

I made my way into the living room—the section of it Carolyn had loved best, not the area where we had occasionally entertained casual guests. The cozy recess was occupied by two facing armchairs, two wooden accent tables, and a shared ottoman between them. Ceiling-to-floor windows on all three sides gave a good view of the wide backyard. After helping ourselves to a glass of our favorite drinks, we would often sit, facing each other, relaxing and chatting, sharing our problems, consoling each other, smoothing over worries, loving each other in sometimes mere silence, mutual presence alone being enough. In later years, I would orient one of the chairs ninety degrees, clockwise or counter, depending on whether Frankie was playing in the living room or in the yard.

I wasn't ready to sit and relax just yet. My little girl remained the priority. And there she was, near the edge of the woods, darting for fallen branches, breaking them, then zigzagging after squirrels and birds, trying to peg the creatures with pieces of wood. I'd allow her an hour of playtime till dinner. I, however, needed something to tide me over.

I left the nook for the nearby bar, which was between

two bookshelves, and poured myself three sips of port. It was the same thirty-year-old tawny Carolyn used to pour herself every Friday evening after a long week spent at the children's hospital. She'd witnessed a different share of horrors in her work. I spilled the blood of once-human beings. She'd dealt with the aftereffects of some onslaught on young bodies, boys and girls suffering in a wide variety of manners. In many ways, she'd been so much stronger than me. Emotionally, for sure. Our daughter seemed en route to taking after her. The girl pouted at times, but it was rare day when I saw her angry.

Still in my jacket, jeans, and gloves, I pondered whether I should take off my boots before kicking back. If Carolyn were here, it wouldn't even be a question; they would've been off in the garage. I set the glass down on the bar and began to kneel down. Then Frankie screamed.

I hit the bar and maybe knocked the glass over as I hustled toward the windows. There was no sign of her out there. I dashed toward the garage. Whatever the situation, I hoped it didn't require a full uniform. The girl knew to be wary of bears and other wild animals; she knew when to run and when to carefully walk away. But there was no telling what else might be in the woods.

I grabbed a full-size semiautomatic pistol and, almost as an afterthought, a microcompact, which I tucked into my waistband before sprinting out of the garage's side door and into the backyard, toward the edge of the woods where I'd last seen her.

"Frankie? *Frankie?*"

No response. I swore if anyone or anything had hurt her in any way, I'd put them through a universe of hurt before putting a few new holes in their head.

I met the edge of the woods and again called her name.

After the slight echo died, I heard a muffled sobbing, forty or maybe fifty feet in.

I adjusted my goggles, readied the pistol, and maneuvered toward the sound.

The sun was setting, and the trees reached high, but there wasn't much of a real need for the enhanced vision the specs allowed. I could see through the woods just fine—though I would need to have my ears checked at some point.

Frankie wasn't sobbing when I found her. She was giggling, almost uncontrollably, with her hands over her mouth. I didn't see the joke. I just saw a stone-faced girl standing next to my daughter. The girl looked just like Carolyn.

3

I holstered the Sig Sauer P226 as I studied the girl. She was wearing a white Sunday school dress, but despite being out in the woods, it was clean and unwrinkled as if she'd just put it on. *She* didn't seem completely clean, though. There were some faint scuff marks on her cheeks and some glittering debris in her hair, and the barrettes in that hair were oddly placed. From the neck down, however, she was a doll.

She was roughly Frankie's age. Had she been out playing alone, or was she lost?

I asked her name and if she lived around here; I got nothing but a blank stare in response. Carolyn's father had been Cuban, and this girl's skin tone betrayed a similar ethnicity. I asked my questions again in Spanish. The girl again said nothing. She wasn't deaf but possibly mute.

Frankie chatted away, at me and the girl, but the girl remained quiet as I ushered them back to the yard, through it, and around to the front of the house, keeping my eyes peeled the entire time. I looked over my shoulder one last time as I ushered them in the front door. No sign of anyone else. I herded both girls past the foyer and into the living room. I didn't invite either to get comfortable.

I pulled out my cellphone. Still no need to take off the gloves; they were infused with touchscreen tech.

"Can we go up to my room and play?" Frankie asked.

I grunted involuntarily before clearing my throat. "I think it's best if you stay right here in front of me." In the house's main area, I could keep a good eye on them, the windows, front door, and the two televisions that doubled as the property's monitors. Besides, there was no way I was letting a stranger into my daughter's bedroom, even if she was a child.

Frankie continued to chat at the girl in what sounded like borderline nonsense to my barely listening ears. My focus was on the girl, who remained tightlipped through it all, standing in place but craning her head around, getting a look at her surroundings. It seemed less casual and more like she was surveying the place.

I pushed the button to put me in direct contact with the authorities—not the local cops, but some men and women who would actually be of some use.

"I found a child," I told the woman who answered, "possibly lost." I gave a description of the girl and the circumstances of my find. The woman promised to send a couple of Heartland agents my way. In the meantime, I shouldn't let the girl leave the house. *No shit.*

I'd kept the girl in my sight the entire time, and she'd said nothing; her expression didn't change. As I reached to pull off my specs, however, something flickered near her head. Was that her?

I left my specs on and adjusted them instead, trying my best to ignore whatever Frankie was babbling about. The girl stared back at me, her brow furrowing slightly, the corners of her mouth twitching almost imperceptibly upward as if daring me to discover her secret and then do something about it.

I didn't exactly discover much. There was something odd about the girl's skin. It had a shifting texture as if it were rapidly switching between an alligator skin's roughness and a metal sheet's smoothness. On top of that, it had an unusual sheen, like oil stains. I couldn't detect the presence of parasites—she apparently wasn't a deviant—but I'd seen enough to worry me.

I motioned toward my daughter. "Frankie, I want you and your friend to come with me."

The girl seemed to understand English, if not speak it. When I moved, she began following me before Frankie did.

I led them down a short hall, into the kitchen, and unbolted the door next to the refrigerator.

"Daddy," Frankie said, "didn't you say I wasn't allowed—"

"*Frankie*"—I gave her my most stern but loving look—"I need you to listen to me, *quietly*. Your new friend here is possibly lost."

"She's not lost. She's here 'cause—"

"Darlin', *please*. I've called some people who can help her find her way home. They'll be here soon. In the meantime, we can play a game to pass the time. This has always been one of daddy's special rooms, one that I never wanted you to play in by yourself, unsupervised. But today it will be a playroom for the three of us, okay?"

It was a terrible ploy, one that I doubted anyone over the age of fourteen would fall for. But time was short, and I couldn't come up with anything more complex; it would only confuse Frankie. Mentioning her sweetwords "play" and "game" was usually enough to get her to go along with whatever. When she smiled and nodded, I knew it had again worked like a charm.

I selected the right key on my ring, unlocked the door, then turned on the light. "Frankie, hold on to the handrail." I took hold of the other girl's right hand in my gloved one and led her down the stairs.

In appearance, it really was just a normal basement, one that hadn't changed much since I'd packed up Carolyn's things—clothes, perfumes, jewelry, and other stuff I couldn't use but that I damn sure wasn't about to throw out. There were no windows down here, and when the door was closed, it was soundproof. There were also no toys.

"Daddy, what are we playing? Where are—"

"Frankie, darlin', I forgot—all the games are upstairs in the closet outside the kitchen. C'mon and help daddy pick something out." I turned to the girl and with a smile said, "We'll be right back."

The girl didn't make a move. If anything, only her eyes followed us out. And Frankie, bless her, didn't ask the most obvious questions as we ascended. She only chattered about the games she wanted to play.

I closed the door behind us, bolted it, locked it, and put the keys in my pocket.

"Daddy," Frankie began, "what—"

"Frankie, listen to me. There's something not right about that girl. You can't be near her, okay? We need to keep her secure down there, *safe* down there, until the people I called get here."

"What's not right about her?"

I heard the tone alerting me that someone was on the front porch a moment before someone knocked on the front door.

The tone alerting me that someone was driving up

hadn't gone off, nor had any of the tones alerting me that someone was walking in the yard. Was the system malfunctioning?

"Frankie, no more questions right now. Go up to your room and lock the door, okay? Can you do that?"

As good a girl as ever, she knew how to follow orders.

She was halfway up the stairs when the knock came again.

I tensed, somewhat happy that I didn't need to scramble to get armed. I cautiously approached the door, ready to unholster either the P226 from under my jacket or the P365 tucked inside my waistband, depending on the threat level. Through the peephole, I saw a woman on the porch looking right back at me as if the door weren't even there.

She was the child's mother. She had her face, with about twenty years added on. The resemblance to Carolyn was uncanny, but the woman's voice was even more unnerving. It seemed as if she were standing right behind me rather than speaking through the reinforced door when she said, "I believe you have something that belongs to me."

Shit. Where the hell were the Agency men? How was I supposed to stall this woman until they arrived?

Or did I even need to stall her? I could've been overreacting. It'd been a tough day and a rough week. I'd spent Sunday tracking two deviants, Monday getting them right where I wanted them, and Tuesday facing them, alone. I'd been through the wringer. This afternoon's tussle had relatively been a walk in the park. But after it all, maybe I just wasn't thinking clearly. I'd had no real chance to get my mind together.

There was definitely something off about the girl, but she wasn't a deviant. The specs had given me some funny readings, but hell, for all I knew the goggles had been damaged during this afternoon's fight—there may've been more to that deviant's static offensive than I'd thought. My specs could've been giving me weird, false readings on a weird but otherwise harmless little girl. Wouldn't have been the first time the goggles had malfunctioned. The girl hadn't given me any trouble. Not at all. She was probably just a damaged kid who couldn't talk and had trouble showing emotions of any kind. And right now, locked in a strange basement, she was probably scared out of her mind. Who knew what torment she was going through, all because of me, an untrusting monster? And what about her mother? In her mind right about now, I was probably nothing short of a kidnapper.

"Just a minute," I said.

I again looked through the peephole. It was a delicate balancing act between being suspicious and being naive. But my instincts rarely failed me. Something was off about this woman as well. Whatever it was, it ran in the family.

I unlocked and unbolted the door. I'd let her in, but if she tried anything funny, I had enough tricks in my jacket to ensure she'd have no time to laugh about it.

I pulled the door open. The stone-faced woman stared at me.

"Can I help you?" I asked.

"There is a little one here," she said. "She is mine. She belongs to me."

The weird fruit certainly didn't fall far from the bizarre tree. I used my specs to examine the woman as I stepped back and invited her in. I got the same funny readings as I'd gotten with her daughter. I'd never seen anything like this before.

"Would you like to have a seat?" I asked. "Can I get you anything to drink?"

The woman remained standing near the door after I closed it. Instead of answering either of my questions, she slowly moved her eyes across the interior, much like her daughter earlier, as if she were casing the place.

"Okay," I muttered. "I'll just be a sec."

I went into the kitchen and unlocked and unbolted the door.

The basement's light was off.

Had I turned it off on my way out? Had I been that absentmindedly cruel? I turned it back on and quickly descended the steps while calling "Little girl?" in the most reassuring tone I could muster. There was no response, of course. But I'd detected no movement either.

I reached the bottom of the stairs and looked around. There was no sign of the girl.

That couldn't be. There was nothing for her to hide behind. All the boxes were stacked close to the walls, with no space between. I'd purposely left the basement uncluttered, planning one day to turn it into a strategy room; I didn't want to move a whole lot of stuff out of it when I did. There were only a couple of folded-up folding chairs, a card table, and the boxes—though some were half-empty, none could fit a preteen girl. I walked the perimeter anyway, touching the boxes as I again called to her in a reassuring tone.

A hunch made me adjust my specs and again look around. Perhaps she'd turned herself invisible?

No, she'd just vanished.

Another hunch made me rush for the stairs. I'd been tricked by someone, but I damn sure wasn't about to be locked in down here.

I made it to the door without even a hint of someone trying to close it on me. I had a brief spell of relief before I wondered what I would tell the kid's mother. No doubt she was already suspicious of me.

I walked back into the living room and knew immediately I should've been more so of her.

She was gone, just like the girl.

A tone sounded, indicating someone was coming up or heading down the driveway. I turned on the television and switched it to monitor mode.

A black sedan parked in front of my garage. The agents had finally arrived.

I opened the front door and stepped onto the porch. Two men stepped out of the car and approached. The clean-shaven one with the square jaw had shoulders and black-frame glasses that were just as square. The slightly shorter one with the five o'clock shadow was carrying a square black briefcase. He had no glasses, just a bird's beady eyes, which were unblinkingly focused on me as he neared. Both men wore gray suits with green pinstripes, both carried at least one concealed firearm, and they walked as if daring me to guess what other deadlies they might be hiding on their persons. These weren't routine agents. They were high-office guys. *Odd.* I hadn't called Essen, my regular contact. I'd called the general private number that was available to current and former HSA employees.

Whatever the hell, I was in no mood to mind my tongue as they stepped onto the porch.

"'Bout damn time," I barked.

We forewent handshakes. Instead, we briefly sized one another up, me giving them both a once-over through my specs. They weren't deviants in disguise, but something about them still picked at my nerves. Maybe it was just the day I was having.

"Can we please step inside, Mr. Sanders?" the one with the glasses said in a low, measured tone.

I pulled off my specs, letting them hang down around my neck, and let them pass. I closed the door behind us.

"Mr. Sanders," said glasses, "I'm Special Agent Martin, and this is Special Agent Collins."

Both now offered their hands. I shook them. I could tell that would be the extent of our mutual civility as Collins gruffly asked, "Where's the girl?"

I sighed as I ran my hand through my thinning hair. "Appears to be gone."

"What the hell does that mean?" Collins asked.

I gave them the whole story.

"Mind if we take a look around?" Martin asked.

I shook my head. He stayed put, but Collins headed directly for the kitchen.

"Mr. Sanders," Martin said, "you may not be aware that we have been grappling with a trafficking problem in the region."

"Human trafficking?" I said. "Of course I'm aware. Didn't you read my file? Don't you know why I joined the Agency in the first place?"

"Yes, we know all about that—and quite enough about you. But this problem, it . . ." His chin dropped a little. "Well, it's taken on different *dimensions*."

"What do you mean?"

"Back when you were with the Agency, there was a lot of talk about Virus carriers who'd formed themselves into gangs."

I nodded. "The Infinite Definite." Most, like the two I'd taken out earlier in the week, operated in cells of two.

"Well, the problem isn't just gangs anymore. Now there are cults. On top of some of their other otherworldly talents, some of these carriers have managed to establish portals, *tunnels* to other realms. Realms where strange and powerful things live. Things we are trying to understand so we can do what we can to make sure they stay in their place. One of these cults has been engaged in some kind of exchange with the beings on the other side."

I cocked my head and squinted at the man. I hoped he wasn't going to say what I didn't want to hear, but I had to ask. "Do you mean—?"

I couldn't get it out, but Martin nodded. "They're trading children."

Goddamned deviants. And to think some in the Agency questioned the philosophy of killing all these diseased shits on sight.

Collins returned, wearing latex gloves. Evidently, the briefcase he'd brought with him wasn't filled with papers but some kind of equipment.

"Ran some tests in the basement," he said. "Something was definitely down there, and it was definitely not of this world."

"How'd it get out?" I asked.

"Don't know exactly, but it left a huge stain when it left. Only the spectrograph picked it up."

I had to get Frankie out of here. We both needed to relocate to a fortified safe cabin in case that thing came back. But how long would we have to stay away? What were the chances of me finding that thing and killing it—it *and* its "mother"?

"What do you two know?" I asked. "How are you tracking these things? Can they be traced? What kills them?"

"I've told you pretty much all we can," Martin said.

"Which has been useless," I said. "I need to know how to *find* and *kill* these things."

"Yeah," Collins said, "we got your meaning the first time."

"Mr. Sanders, we know that, since your 'retirement,' the Agency has allowed you certain freedoms."

"You kill," Collins said. "And that's *all* you do. We prefer to monitor, capture if we can, and study—which, in the end, is more beneficial."

"How is it beneficial to let murderous plague carriers live freely among us?"

"Not all are dangerous," Martin said. "Look at your average gang member. Many engage in criminal behavior, but most don't engage in violent acts. Some are actually rehabilitated."

"Isn't that what your old running buddy Marcus Graham used to do back when he was an agent?" Collins asked with more than a hint of a sneer.

I gave him a cold, hard look. "Don't you dare mention his name. Not to me. Not in this house."

Martin began, "Mr. Sanders—"

"You *can't* rehabilitate deviants," I said. "There's no cure for what they've got. All of them are potential murderers or rapists. The worst of them go for the *mind* first. And when *they* organize into gangs, they ramp up their activity, taking it to extremes. And now we're talking *cults*?"

"Guilty and never proven innocent, huh?" Collins said. "That's your entire worldview? It's a wonder you're not in the state assembly."

Yeah, there was a reason I was asked to "retire" from the Agency. But there was also a reason why I was allowed "certain freedoms," as Martin put it. What had happened with

Graham's kids had been an anomaly. But giving an inch to an adult or even a teenage deviant was bad philosophy.

"Studying the living ones," Martin said, "helps us learn how to protect and defend ourselves against them if we need to while, you know, they're still alive. The dead ones won't be attacking. Now, don't get me wrong. I respect what you do—"

"Sure as shit doesn't sound like it."

"Well, with all due respect, you were a black ops guy, out in the dirt every day and night. Black Peacemakers have to be a little touched"—he tapped a finger on his temple—"to be effective. Now, as a Designated Hitter, it's the same story with you, just a different chapter. But some of us have a more scientific perspective. These so-called deviants are not zombies or vampires from some dumb sci-fi movie. They're actual human beings who, thanks to a virus, have managed to acquire supernatural abilities, one of the most unique and important being to access other dimensions, other realms of reality. If we can *understand* that ability, in the long run it may somehow be used to benefit humanity. But we won't be able to understand how they do the things they do if they're all dead."

I'm sure he sounded sensible to some, and I'm sure he was well meaning. But to me it all sounded a little too much like, "We should let a group of terrorists experiment with chemicals. Sure, they may develop a bomb, or they may find a cure for cancer." I was the impatient sort, the type of guy who preferred to judge people either by what they've done or by their inclinations. The content of their character. I'd never encountered a Virus carrier over the age of ten who wasn't out to rape, mutilate, murder, or engage in some other sort of nonsensical mayhem. The deviants didn't even see what they were doing as bad; they simply claimed to be creating some kind of "higher art." I'd no patience for that nonsense. Maybe if they were all confined to Broadway and Hollywood and promised to stay there, I'd be willing to back off a bit.

"You may not know us, Mr. Sanders," Martin said. "But we know you well: all the business of your days as a cop, agent, sanctioned hunter, and even the most recent diversionary business involving your crusade in the name of he-you-do-not-want-named."

Collins grunted. "You're lucky you're not rotting under a black site prison for some of the dirty shit you've done."

"And I regret none of it," I said—not 100 percent truthfully but 90 percent there.

Collins raised an eyebrow. "Oh yeah? What if we told you that a strain of the Virus was recently discovered in human remains, 4,500 years old, from the Bronze Age? What then, tough guy?"

"I'd say show me the proof, smart ass."

"We can't," Martin said. "Not yet. But soon the evidence will be out there among those who have a need to know. Proof that the Virus wasn't a creation of the government. It predates the United States by quite a bit."

"Doesn't prove someone didn't rediscover it," I said, "and try to weaponize it."

"You're a damn fool," Collins growled as he tightened his eyes even further and began to close the distance between us. "Your old pal Marcus Graham infected *you* with a virus, a psychological one, an insanity that pushed you to finish off his work of killing government agents—two good, faithful agents—and other allies of Heartland Security. Those same agents and allies told you things under torture that you misinterpreted, pushing you even further down the path of being Graham's running dog. Someone with your experience should know, Frank—torture doesn't work."

There was about two feet of space between me and Collins. His nostrils were flaring. I flexed my fingers, but I wouldn't strike the first blow. Nor was I going to take a step back. I simply took a breath and shifted my gaze to Martin. "Let me take a shot in the dark here. No more Essen, right? You two are going to be on my ass from now on."

Martin said nothing. The corners of Collins's mouth upturned slightly as he took a step back. Before I could invite them to get the hell out, both men began toward the door. "We'll be in touch," Martin said, "if we hear any more about happenings in this area. Maybe you could extend us the same courtesy?"

I followed them into the foyer. "What the hell's your game?"

"We're dedicated to studying these traffickers and all those involved."

"And I may now be involved in some way of which I'm unaware," I said. "Is that it?"

They exchanged glances briefly before Martin simply said, "Good night, Mr. Sanders."

I followed the men outside and stood on the porch until they drove away. The sun was a memory, but I didn't see any stars. No way I even could. There was an asperitas cloud formation above—thick and roiling, almost like the sea. A downpour could come at any moment.

I stepped back inside, locked the door behind me, and called for Frankie.

No response.

I headed for the stairs and called again.

Same silence.

I hustled up to her room.

I knocked first, not only because I'd told her to lock the door but also because I respected her privacy. When my knocking wasn't answered, however, I turned the knob and rushed in.

Gone.

Goddamn it.

4

My thoughts raced one another, passing through a variety of scenarios as the room spun around me. One scenario stood out more than any other: That "woman" had snatched Frankie when I was in the basement. I was certain of this a moment before my eyes rested on the dresser's top.

There was a postcard with a picture of the nearest national forest. I'd taken Frankie there a few times, but we'd never bought a postcard. I picked it up, turned it over, and saw a series of numbers. Geographic coordinates.

This was more than torn hair or a discarded label. This wasn't a clue that required a detective. This was an engraved invitation.

I stuffed the card into my back pocket and ran for the garage.

No sense in calling the Agency. They'd just send out the same shitheads who'd just left, two dolts intent on capturing these vermin. I'd call them after I killed every deviant, cult follower, and *whatever* that I could get my damn hands on. The agents could examine the corpses.

Collins had said that all I do is kill, as if there were no rhyme or reason behind my motives. Maybe he hadn't studied my file closely enough. The Agency didn't give the perks I had to all its retirees, not even those who'd been asked to leave. It was more than the fact that I continued a beneficial mission when it wasn't politically feasible for me to do so while on their payroll. It was that I was damned effective in achieving desired results for the greatest good.

If civilians knew about deviant-hunters at all, most would probably assume my kind wore black. But my battle-dress uniform was silver and gold. Neither black nor camouflage made sense with all the optical tricks the deviants could pull. The special material, however, did make it harder for them to see me, if not impossible. In their eyes I would appear as a blur rather than a solid object. The material made the uniform especially resistant if not fully impervious to bullets, blades, fire, and the types of electromagnetic onslaught most deviants would unleash as their first and second lines of offense. I laid aside my specs and put on a more comfortable pair of prescription glasses, a pair that synced exceptionally well with my helmet's visor.

I attached my belt and tactical vest, checking and rechecking every pouch, pocket, and holster, making sure they held what I night need: Skrapnel capsules, Pixie Dust eggs, syringes filled with liquid metal, a P320 X-Five, an ADS gun, a vamper, a gunlight, and all the rest. I loaded a backpack with stuff I couldn't hold anywhere else on my person. My body was ready. I turned my attention to The Machine.

Much bigger and tougher than the average Hummer, the silver-and-black vehicle had tinted, reinforced windows. The personal-protection vehicle had been designed to help defend against everything from mines to firearms, even though deviants rarely used such offensive measures. Their bodies, minds, and language were their most potent weapons. I'd often fantasized about using The Machine to mow a few of them down; funny that such opportunities had been few and far between. Lately, the vehicle had mostly served as a secure transport for Frankie and me and as a repository for extra weapons, ammunition, and a spare outfit.

I settled myself in the driver's seat and pushed the buttons that would open the garage and then secure the house as I sped like a demon down the driveway. I headed in the general direction of the forest. At the first red light that I couldn't safely run, I took the time to put the coordinates into my GPS. When I had a better sense of where I was going, I increased my speed.

Odd that it wasn't raining yet, but the clouds were just as heavy and agitated as they had been before. Thankfully, they didn't screw with my GPS.

Within twenty minutes, the roads pulled me into the woods. I doubted I could ever make it on the professional circuit of racers, but I handled the curves well enough while maintaining a good clip up and down hills. The farther I went, the less opposing traffic I encountered, but The Machine's headlights were losing the battle with the darkness, which seemed more overwhelming with each half mile traveled.

I crested a hill and took a sharp curve left, only to see a deer standing in the road. I turned the wheel and slammed on the brakes. The animal didn't move. A moment before I hit it, I saw it wasn't a deer at all.

It was too bulky and too tall to be a deer, but the head did have antlers—*both* of the heads had antlers. And I only caught a glimpse of it, but its tail made me think of a scorpion.

The passenger's side of The Machine hit the creature like a wall. The vehicle had crashed into actual walls before, usually not by accident. It had rarely been a problem. But never before had I seen the passenger's side crumple in and the windows shatter. There was even a slump in the rear as if one or both tires had gone flat.

The creature poked one of its noses into the passenger's side window. The byzantine configuration of antlers prevented it from coming in too far, but I saw enough. A noxious, mossy-green vapor wafted from the nostrils. I did what I could to hold my breath as I looked into the creature's swirling red-and-blue eyes; I saw what it wanted me to see. The cult was near, and they were indeed waiting for me.

The creature backed up a little and, making sure I got the message, whipped its body around. I heard metal shearing and a crash, one right after the other. The damned creature had used its tail to cut the roof clean off The Machine and toss it onto the road. By choice or chance, it had spared my head. Both of *its* heads turned to look at me before it bolted into the woods.

I got out of the vehicle. A quick check verified a back tire was flat. I could maybe fix it, and maybe The Machine would still run despite its condition, but I couldn't take it off the road. The forest was too dense, and the creature had obviously wanted me to follow it on foot. I'd little choice. I had to follow the cultists' rules, for now. But I rethought my rash decision to leave the authorities out of this until it was all over. Emotions overwhelming my intellect would ensure the mission's failure.

Whoever or whatever had snatched Frankie was playing me. They'd left the postcard on purpose, and if I'd have contacted the authorities before heading out, my backup would've headed to a spot far different from where the creature was drawing me. They'd thought this through. I'd compliment the smart bastards before I dusted them.

Everything on the dash was still working, thankfully. I pushed the red distress button next to the radio, which would eventually be picked up by the local HSA field office. I did the same with my phone; an alert would probably go directly to my current contacts, who'd be able to pinpoint my exact location. But I couldn't wait around for anyone. I'd already lost precious time.

It took effort, but I managed to steer the vehicle to the side of the road, just far enough out of the way so that no cruising innocents would crash into it. I then grabbed my backpack, rechecked my accessories, added a flare gun and two rockets, and then rushed into the forest, adjusting my helmet's visor to make it easier to spot fresh tracks. With the frequency I was using, the creature's prints seemed etched in luminous paint.

But there was something strange. The prints I saw matched those of claws and hooves, the former on the forelegs and the latter on the hind legs. And the creature was agile. The crazy path I followed made no sense for any animal I'd ever seen. It zagged and zigged as if it were part crab; at some points, it even seemed to climb halfway up a few trees before jumping off, circling, and cutting in a new direction.

I wouldn't have believed my visor was giving me the correct info if I hadn't gotten within fifty or so feet of the creature and seen it moving in such an erratic manner.

It froze when it spotted me. My right hand itched to draw my Sig Sauer P320 and plug it. But I had an inkling bullets would be useless. Instead, I kept up a cautious approach.

I'd gotten halfway when it moved again, this time more

straightforward. I hustled after it, focusing on it until it dashed into a clearing and I saw the shadowy figure it was running toward.

I slowed, drawing the Sig with one hand and adjusting my visor with the other, switching to a different sort of night vision. I wanted to ensure there was only one figure. Satisfied, I switched to a cleaner mode, which gave me a clear picture of what was before me but at the same time protected me from being blinded in case a bright ball of dazzling light was tossed my way.

The two-headed creature I'd followed awkwardly circled the figure three times before hunkering down to rest at the figure's left side; both of the creature's heads remained focused on me. I hadn't been counting on the element of surprise, but I wasn't about to bound out into the clearing like a jackrabbit. I kept to the edge, keeping cover behind a maple tree.

It was a fairly big clearing; the figure seemed to be standing smack dab in the middle of it. It had some girth, but I couldn't pick up any other features. It appeared to be wearing a pitch-black cloak. And the heavy sky above helped preserve its secrecy.

It surely had a better view of me than I did of it. I figured, at this point, a more direct route was the best to take.

I fiddled with my helmet's voice changer to amplify my words, giving them an appropriately grim tone of authority. "Who are you?"

The figure raised its arms to pull back its hood. I adjusted the setting of my visor.

It was the woman.

I stepped out from behind the trees and aimed my pistol at her head as I approached. "Where is my daughter?"

The woman pulled open her cloak. For a moment, I saw nothing but a black void, then out stepped my daughter and this woman's daughter, hand in hand, wearing identical black dresses.

I was within thirty feet. I had a bead on the woman's forehead, right between the eyes. The kids were close but clear—and I've never had a better reason in my life not to miss. I pulled the trigger.

I heard the report, but her head didn't whip back as expected. She didn't even flinch.

But I hadn't missed.

I pulled the trigger again, twice more, each time even more sure of my aim. Getting the same result, I lowered my weapon, slid it into the vest's holster.

I adjusted the changer, modifying my voice to one more human. "Frankie, darlin', come to daddy. *Run* to daddy."

Frankie didn't move. She was unusually silent. Expressionless, like the other girl.

I could run up and snatch her, but then what?

"Out of ideas?" The woman's voice had an odd echo to it. The effect wasn't due to her surroundings. It was like her words were being spoken from deep within the pit of her and had to travel a ways to get up and out of her mouth.

"No. I have a few more." With both hands, I reached into the side pockets of my backpack, retrieving a rocket flare and another gun. The woman neither turned her head nor flinched when I fired.

The rockets would travel about a thousand feet up into the air. The flare would eventually help reinforcements find me. More immediately, I'd hoped it would distract her.

No such luck. The ocean of clouds seemed to redirect the light, momentarily raining down beams of pale, reddish light. The woman's gaze remained fixed on me as I tilted my head upward, catching glimpses of figures in the surrounding trees. Tall figures.

I adjusted my visor and spotted three, four . . . *ten* in all as I turned in a circle. They were a few dozen feet from the ground and wearing cloaks similar to the woman's—cloaks that covered all their features. But I saw eyes as intense as red-hot coals, shining from out of the void under their hoods.

Cultists. Just a different brand of deviants.

My flare probably wouldn't bring immediate assistance, but it—or something—triggered a change in the sky. The clouds parted in small patches, allowing thin beams of bright moonlight to reign. As the beams became more copious, the figures in the trees took on new appearances. They pulled the moonlight *to* them, refined it, and threaded it through the late-spring leaves surrounding their bodies. The figures now seemed like large, demonic owls, each more than ten feet in length. With raised arms they used the moonlight to stitch their cloaks to the leaves, making it appear they had wings of cloth and foliage, and wingspans well over a dozen feet long.

The tips of their "wings" touched. They formed an unbroken circle as their faces slowly revealed themselves: large, glowing eyes, jutting noses, and chins with sharp, prominent teeth in between.

Ugliness, whether real or illusory, didn't intimidate me. Neither did size nor spring's leaves. But hell, I was more than ready for *fall.*

I backed away from the woman, the two girls, and the creature who'd led me here, none of whom showed any sign of wanting to move. I readied the ADS weapon I'd kept holstered on my thigh as I ran toward the nearest cultist.

Handheld ADS weapons were still in the highly experimental stage, not available for use by anyone at any level in the armed forces. How I managed to procure one was a secret even my most-trusted didn't know, but the one I managed to procure not only excited the water and fat molecules in a target's skin, effectively acting as a heat ray, it also emitted a high-frequency sound that entered a target's ears and somehow went straight toward the bone marrow, reacting with it, making a target feel as if their bones were shaking themselves to pieces. The latter function is probably why the weapons were still in the experimental stage; it wasn't an intended consequence.

Whatever the outcome, my suit would protect me, and distance would protect my daughter. But I made damn sure to get as close as I could to the cloak-wearing cultist who would be my first target.

I aimed and pulled the trigger. Even if his cloak protected his skin, it couldn't fully protect his ears.

I wasn't sure if he was hurt or just pissed, but after shaking in his branches a bit, he leaped down and moved straight toward me. I reholstered the weapon, ducked, rolled, and came up to a knee, hands at the ready to swiftly retrieve two Skrapnel capsules with one hand while slipping the other into the clawed silver knuckle I kept in my belt. I didn't know all that this freak could do, but I'd have to bank that my suit could withstand it.

As he closed in, I sprang to my feet and rushed for him. We were set to collide; he seemed set to engulf me in his cloak. Instinct pushed me to switch one capsule to the clawed hand and fling it toward his center. He took it and shuddered as I lowered my shoulder and went straight for the middle. He'd seen me coming, but I still seemed to catch him off guard. I got one leg behind his as I thrust the sharp knuckle toward his chin. He jerked back, tripped on my leg, and lost his balance. My claw caught at the cloak's clasp around his neck and severed it. I grabbed his neck with the same hand. His struggle to regain balance caused his cloak to loosen up enough for me to see skin, and he was uncovered long enough for me to smack the remaining Skrapnel capsule against his cheek.

Whatever his abilities, whatever his beliefs, he had enough flesh to feel that. His scream caused half of the other cultists to come swooping down.

These cloaked fools tried to manipulate the moonlight and the lack of it in all manners of ways to make them appear to be some *things* they weren't. A simple adjustment of my helmet's visor allowed me to see through all the illusions. But the cloaks were still a problem.

I unholstered the ADS again and ran toward the approaching cultists who were farthest from my unmoving daughter. The weapon stopped one in his tracks and caused another to collapse, but before it could do a thing to a third, I felt a pulsating sting inside my hand—as if mites were gnawing on the nerves—before it went numb. I dropped the weapon and turned.

The cultist who'd been behind me cracked his arm against the side of my helmet.

The blow *cracked* the helmet. The visor now gave me double vision. It worsened when the cultist hit me again.

I threw myself forward, shoving all my weight into him. I couldn't see everything that happened, but I felt him grabbing and tossing me. I counted to three before I hit the ground.

With nothing broken but plenty bruised, I set both hands to work on removing my helmet.

When I managed to get it off, I saw that all the cultists had descended and were closing in, wrapping themselves in all manners of hallucinatory visions. My training helped me to see and recognize them for what they were, but that was about it. My regular glasses wouldn't be able to penetrate the illusions or pick up anything that had turned invisible.

I looked for my ADS, the one thing that seemed to be effective without me having to get up close and personal. There was no sign of it.

Fine. I'd have to go back to basics.

I ran toward the nearest target. I'd tackle, hold him down, pull my semiauto, and fire a few rounds into his brain. And when I ran out of bullets, I'd switch to the syringes, jabbing them into the temples of these cultists.

What had I to lose? They wanted *me.* I realized that. If they'd simply wanted Frankie, they wouldn't have left a trail for me to follow. But I didn't care what they wanted. And I had no intention of letting them have anything.

I closed in on a cultist and dipped my shoulder. He opened his cloak wide and stood still. Then, I was still—lost in a void of pure black.

With the other cultist, I'd felt a body. Was that thanks to the Skrapnel? Whether it was or not, with this one, there was *nothing.*

I saw nothing and felt nothing for who-the-hell-knew-how-long until my whole sense of being was jerked and tossed like garbage onto solid ground. I was again in front of the woman, her daughter and mine, and the two-headed creature. My uniform was gone. I'd been stripped down to my undergarments: stretchable combat shirt and base-layer shorts.

I got to my feet and looked around. The cultists had deserted. They may have been back up in the trees, but I sure as hell couldn't see them. The holes in the clouds had healed themselves. Without my specs, glasses, or helmet, my vision was limited in these conditions. But all I needed to see—*wanted* to see—was right in front of me.

I tried to steady my breath as I looked at Frankie. Eyes wide, face unexpressive, no hint of breathing—she looked like a doll. I shifted my eyes to the woman.

"We do not have much time," she said. "You have wasted plenty, and I must take my leave soon."

Every muscle in my upper body tensed. "What the *hell* are you? What have you done to my daughter?"

"Have you ever considered what happens when you die?" the woman asked.

I again looked at Frankie. *Oh God—was she . . . ?*

"Ten years ago in this realm," the woman said, "there were accidents. There was a rift between our realms. Some from my realm had inadvertently but briefly crossed into yours, at various points, unintentionally causing the deaths of some of your people. Where I am from, what your people call 'souls' are not merely ideas; they *mean* something, and those meanings are like jewels."

Souls had always meant something to me, worth *more* than any gemstones. Deviants didn't have any souls; they had allowed theirs to be devoured gluttonously by evil ideas. But this "woman" wasn't exactly a deviant, so—"What are you saying?"

"I was one of those who accidentally crossed over. When I did, I caused the death of a woman. One whom you knew."

Carolyn.

The woman seemed to read my thoughts. "I come from a realm of light. But during the collision, pieces of her soul were mixed with my being. With some manipulation, they allow me to exist in your realm solidly but temporarily. The woman, she is dead to this world, but she still exists. She simply no longer exists in a form one of your limited comprehension can understand."

My chest heaved. I didn't want to ask it outright. I couldn't take it, not after what I'd been through today. Heaven, Hell—I believed in them, *both* of them, but I didn't want stone-cold confirmation, not *yet*. Not with Frankie here. I wasn't ready to take it. I had to skip over the obvious, inhale deeply, and simply ask, "Why are you here now?"

"It took me some time to make my way back to this realm—and more to locate what was mine. When I crossed over the first time, I was not alone. But the one with whom I came is not the one with whom I left."

My head involuntarily and slowly shook from one side to the other. My intuition had amped up, and I hated what it was telling me.

"The one you have referred to as your daughter for the past ten years is not what she seems. She has taken on a remarkable resemblance to a human being, growing at the proper rate, acting in the proper way. But she is not yours. You have only believed so because pieces of your daughter's soul were mixed with this one, giving you just enough feeling of connection."

My eyes flicked to the other girl then back to the woman's. "You're lying. All this—you're a *damned* liar. That's *not* possible."

"Look at these two, closely." She raised her arms and pointed her index fingers downward, like swords of Damocles, over the scalps of both girls. "Use whatever abilities or tricks or rationality you have at your disposal, but think on it hard. Which one is more likely yours?"

This was all some kind of twisted game. Some *mind-fucking* game.

One woman, two girls. Two of the three strongly resembled Carolyn, while the third was her flesh and blood, *our* flesh and blood, or flesh, blood, and . . .

My temples throbbed. Random joints seemed suddenly replaced by jellyfish, wobbling while sending stinging shocks throughout my nervous system. In my eyes, the two girls were now more like each other than the girl with Carolyn's face was like the woman. I felt dizzy, but somewhere within—*deep* within—I felt drawn more to the girl, not to Frankie. It was . . . that *face.*

"That one . . ." I hesitantly raised my finger to point at her as well. "This one is . . . she's . . ."

"*Yours,*" the woman said. "Kept safe in my realm all this time. She is not quite herself, but she will awaken fully into her own once I have left this realm."

I shook my head, though I felt like nodding. There was something in the girl, something *pulling* me. A magnetic quality. "What do you want from me?" I muttered.

"Your permission," the woman said. "To make the exchange. Without your assent, I cannot take back what is mine. But you will also not keep what is rightfully yours."

The long day had caught up to me. Fatigue had crept in steadily, but now it had imbued me to such a point that I felt I was losing balance, both physical and mental.

"I . . . I need some time to absorb all this. I need to—"

"*Make* a decision," the woman said. "It is nearing midnight. I will take my leave then and take what I brought with me, unless I have your permission."

Nearing midnight. Nearly naked and under an oppressive sky, I had no idea how near to midnight we really were. Worse, stripped of my phone and uniform, it would be harder for my backup to find me. Not that they would do me much good at this point. They couldn't harm the woman any more than I could. And the cultists, no doubt still keeping a close eye over all this, would probably subdue them as easily as they had me.

I looked at the girls, who were indistinguishable save for their faces. One was Carolyn's. The other's was unique, neither mine nor my wife's. It hadn't been the surgery, as I'd always assumed. Those scratches had been signs of more than a car accident. Maybe that guy I—

Maybe I shouldn't have done what I'd done. I'd been so sure at the time; now I was sure he was as much an innocent victim as my wife. Both my wife and that man had a soul. Hopefully, his ended up somewhere peaceful. I still needed to find a way to apologize and find a piece of redemption. I didn't always understand my God, but I understood now that the deity was pushing me to take a first step in righting a grave wrong. Transcending one's own skin into angelhood —it meant expanding the soul and looking beyond base feelings like revenge, vanity, selfishness. My choice, now, was obvious.

I nodded slowly before meeting the woman's eyes.

"You have my permission," I said, "to take what's yours and to leave what's mine."

The lower half of the woman's face twisted grotesquely into something resembling a grin; her eyes flared as she raised her arms to the sky. The clouds above separated to form a wide, gaping hole. The unhampered brightness of a full moon shone down, illuminating the entire clearing.

It was more than mere moonlight. The clearing was as bright as a meadow at noon on a cloudless summer day, but the light was tainted, grayish.

The girls ceased holding hands, dropping them to their sides. The woman put her hand on Frankie's shoulder, and she took a step backward. The woman lowered her hands to open her cloak wide. My eyes welled up as Frankie silently stepped backward into that black abyss, disappearing. The woman closed her cloak. Her face was again expressionless, yet her image and that of the two-headed creature shimmered.

I felt I'd made the right decision, but the woman's grin bothered me. I was impelled to get off some parting shots.

"I may have given you permission for this exchange," I said, "but you don't have my forgiveness for causing the death of my wife."

"I did not ask for it." The woman's voice now seemed to come from the heavens, not from her body at all. "The death of your wife was unintentional. Where I am from, I—like you—am considered a hunter. When hunting, accidents are bound to occur. Unlike you, however, I am no intentional murderer of innocents."

The woman's form appeared as bluish-gray wisps, each strand of smoky light fighting hard to maintain a human's form and just as hard to break free from it.

"Murderer" maybe—but certainly not an intentional one of innocents. I wouldn't debate that point. Her other words were more puzzling. "What do *you* hunt? Especially with a young daughter in tow, putting her at risk when the accidents happen?"

"I hunt stars," the voice said, "the unblemished essence of human children. We do not kill; we capture. And we have neither daughters nor sons. We have pets. *Trackers.*"

The woman's and creature's wisps dissipated in the moonlight, and the clouds repaired themselves, again leaving me in darkness with the girl.

I met her eyes. She met mine.

Though fatigue had almost completely overtaken me and my legs felt as if they could give at any moment, I remained still, frozen, as the "girl" shifted.

I heard no bones breaking. There were no ruptures in the skin. No blood of any sort appeared. Most amazing of all, there was no screaming, not even an anguished gurgle, just a subtle hiss as the girl fell to all fours. Her face elongated, and her hair and skin became something like fiery fur; her hands and feet gnarled in on themselves and unfolded as claws. Her backside sprouted a tail, and her dress ripped and re-formed into a black bat's wings.

When it was all said and done, I was gazing at a bister-fawn-and-black creature that primarily resembled a fanged deer, with the size and apparent muscles of a Great Dane. There were no antlers, just two sharp tricolored horns between the eyes—one at least ten inches long, the other under it about half the length—seemingly both able and ready to gore an enemy. The wings looked powerful enough to lift and carry the entire body at a good clip yet flexible enough to finesse the same body out of perilous situations. The eyes were too terrible to contemplate, but they wouldn't turn away from mine. And I couldn't turn away.

We weren't locked in a death stare. This was something else. Something familiar.

I reached out and laid my hand on her head, just behind the longer horn. She made her first sound, guttural and beautiful at once—and, again, *familiar*.

I knelt down and smiled, moving my hand under her chin. She couldn't smile, but she seemingly did the equivalent as her eyes blazed. My body shook from its core outward as I felt myself being lifted and carried high above the clearing. As she whisked us up and away, I glanced down and saw two or three figures entering the clearing from the woods. I couldn't tell if they were agents—and I couldn't have cared less.

THE BLACK-PURPLE LIQUID on my palate was almost indescribable—powerful but with great finesse. It was a vintage port from the end of the twentieth century. I'd never tasted anything like it before, but I'd been ready for a change.

I set the glass down on the accent table and leaned back in the easy chair as I read the incoming message on my phone. A few days ago, I had called in one of my few remaining favors and had my Agency resources locate the offspring of the man I'd wrongly killed. He had two kids: a son and a daughter in their early teens. I'd asked about setting up some kind of scholarship or trust fund for them, but that wasn't in my connection's power. I'd have to look toward other connections, other powers. Martin and Collins had been skulking around the premises; maybe it was finally time to invite them in to chat and see if they could handle this for me. In the meantime, on this late evening, I was having a true partner handle something just as important.

All the lights were off. The house and property were secure, and moonlight poured in through the nook's windows. But I didn't need the wan light to see Karol—presently in her "human" form—dancing about the living room, leaping and bouncing from furniture to coffee table to floor, twisting and turning in midair. She was happy we'd been reunited, but that celebration had nearly extinguished itself over the last several days. Now she was happy we'd made a breakthrough in our research. She approached me now, chattering up a storm.

She didn't speak with words but with pictures and—during her really animated moods—moving images. Over the past week and a half, we'd managed to establish an imperfect but fairly effective method of communication.

As she became acclimated to this world, and with a little assistance from some of my more high-tech equipment, Karol learned to conjure more complex images, giving pictorial if sometimes only symbolic responses to my words and other verbal expressions of the things weighing heavily on my mind. *Hell*, at times, she practically read my mind. And ever since that strange day we'd met—or, rather, had been reunited—she seemed as ambitious as I was.

There'd be no more taking out random Virus carriers. There'd be no more letting my base passions get the best of me. From now on, I was going to be focused. And Karol seemed just as focused as I was in wanting to locate the cultists. We wanted to find out their true role in our reunion. We wanted to know their endgame.

Presently, of all the images Karol was conjuring, she made two more prominent than the others and pushed them toward me: an image of one of the cultists without her hood—a dark-skinned woman with glowing orange eyes and flickering green pupils—and the image of the Pentagon, just outside of Washington, DC.

"Good work, darlin'." I tapped my right index finger to my forehead. She reciprocated with her left index finger. "Now head upstairs and get some rest. First thing in the morning, the hunt's on."

ABOUT THE SERIES

When their bodies are overwhelmed by an onslaught of parasites that feed on blood and light, most victims of the White Fire Virus die quickly but in excruciating pain. They could be considered the lucky ones. Those who survive continue to live on in physical and psychological torment; they also find themselves endowed with a range of supernatural abilities. Many of these survivors consider themselves angels, potential saviors of humanity. Others want nothing less than the death of God. And there are a few who are even more ambitious.

Eve of Light is a dark metaphysical fantasy—philosophical, intense, action-packed, and *surreal*.

The Core Novels

BloodLight: The Apocalypse of Robert Goldner
Broken Angels (Eve of Light Book I)
Divinities, Entangled (Eve of Light Book II)

The Deviant-Hunter Stories

Deviant-Hunter: Blood Oath
Deviant-Hunter, Killer of Saints
Deviant-Hunter's Sabbath

Other Stories on the Fringe

FoolKillers
The Lark
Heaven's Gun
Knotty & Ice
Rogue Beauty

ABOUT THE AUTHOR

Harambee K. Grey-Sun writes under the broad umbrella of speculative fiction. He integrates elements of fantasy, horror, noir, black humor, and science fiction into his work, spinning tales that are dark, surreal, mysterious, grotesque, at times challenging, and—some would even say—blasphemous. His dark metaphysical fantasy series, Eve of Light, examines the dark nature of God and what it really means to be human.

For more information:

Click Here for Author's Website
www.harambeegreysun.com

ALSO BY HARAMBEE K. GREY-SUN

Standalone Stories

Beholder

Love Among the Ultramoderns

Unfair Play

Last Contact

The Lure

The *EVE OF LIGHT* Series

The Novels

BloodLight: The Apocalypse of Robert Goldner (*Prequel*)

Broken Angels (*Book I*)

Divinities, Entangled (*Book II*)

The Novellas

Deviant-Hunter: Blood Oath

Deviant-Hunter, Killer of Saints

Deviant-Hunter's Sabbath

The Short Stories

Hell's Brood (*A Collection*)

BY HARAMBEE GREY-SUN

Poetry

Spring's Fall (Autumn Numbers * Book I)

Wine Songs, Vinegar Verses

www.ingramcontent.com/pod-product-compliance
Lightning Source LLC
Chambersburg PA
CBHW071013120726
47910CB00004B/1506